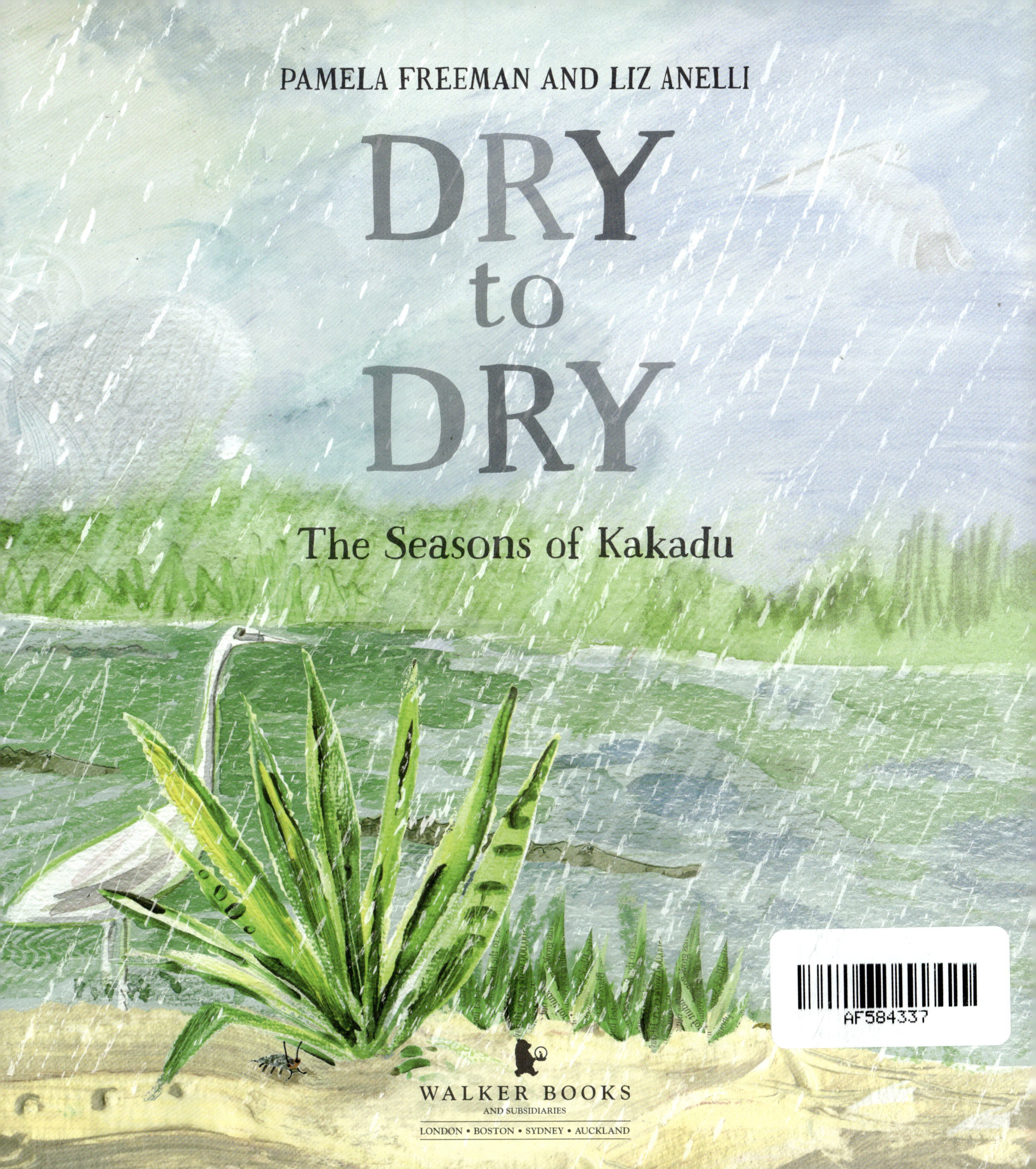

PAMELA FREEMAN AND LIZ ANELLI

DRY to DRY

The Seasons of Kakadu

WALKER BOOKS
AND SUBSIDIARIES
LONDON • BOSTON • SYDNEY • AUCKLAND

It is the Dry.

Over the plains and cliffs and rivers of Kakadu, in northern Australia, the air hangs heavy.

It's hot and very humid.

The rivers have shrunk down to creeks; the edges of the lakes are banks of mud where crocodiles **sunbake**.

Look closer: there is a northern long-necked turtle that has buried itself safely in the cool mud, **waiting** until the **Wet comes.**

In northern Australia, there are two main seasons: wet and dry. In the middle of the year, during the Dry, it rains very rarely. That period lasts from May to October. The Wet comes after that and lasts until April.

A flock of little curlews a thousand strong arrives from the Arctic Circle and settles on the grasslands near the rivers. Other birds are coming too:

snipes,

godwits,

sharp-tailed sandpipers

and more.

Kakadu has more than 280 bird species, the most of any area in Australia. Thousands of birds from Europe and Asia come to Kakadu to avoid the northern winter. Some fly more than 5000 kilometres!

In the *Pityrodia* bushes, the rare Leichhardt's grasshoppers **hatch and begin to chomp** on the bitter leaves. They will go through seven stages before they reach full growth, **moulting their skin** at each stage.

High in the sky over the Yellow Water wetlands, the red-tailed black cockatoos **flock noisily to their night-time home**, a grove of eucalypts, before afternoon storm clouds gather.

Lightning and thunder!

The first kiss of rain on the blazingly dry grasslands.

Although storms bring some rain in November and December, it is only just enough to start the creeks flowing again.

Two magpie larks **sing a duet** together while **building their round nest** of mud and grass. The red lily sends up sweet-smelling flowers from the billabongs and wetlands.

In spring and early summer the waters of Kakadu begin to spread and watercourses are washed clean – but the water is sometimes acidic, and kills fish in the shrunken billabongs.

The long-legged jabiru **stalks the wetlands,** seeking out eels and frogs it can take back to its babies in a huge old nest high up in a banyan tree.

About twenty-five frog species live in Kakadu and they are an important source of food for many creatures, including birds, snakes, fish and turtles. They all eat frogs, either when they are tadpoles or fully developed adults.

Termites build their mounds up – some are **three times** as high as a grown man. Other animals live in and on the mounds.

Look! A gecko has found shelter from the hot summer sun.

Termite mounds grow up to six metres above ground. The mounds are built to keep the termite nests beneath them cool and are made of mud, termite saliva and pieces of dried grass or faeces. They can last for one hundred years or more.

Crack!

Hiss!

The monsoon begins, pelting down warm summer rain for hours. Wetlands spread across the low-lying ground.

This is the Wet.

During monsoon season, it rains around two out of every three days. Some days, more than eight centimetres of rain can fall. Humidity is high – over eighty per cent on most mornings.

Crocodiles leave their riverbanks
and go hunting.

Kakadu has both freshwater crocodiles and the much bigger saltwater crocodiles that live on the beaches and in the estuaries of the rivers. Crocodiles eat birds, frogs, fish and crustaceans.

Spear grass can grow up to two metres during the wet season. The temperature is high, there is enough light despite the clouds, and water is plentiful: perfect conditions for fast growth.

The spear grass **shoots up**, delighting in the constant rain and heat. Within it, birds, snakes, frogs and lizards **nest and scurry.**

Creeks and rivers swell and break their banks.
Out across the plains,
silver sheets of water spread,
joining creek to creek
until half of Kakadu becomes a wetland.

The plateau's towering cliffs become thunderous waterfalls. Below them, at night, the chorus of frogs is deafening.

In the paperbarks, the brush-tailed tuan hunts for centipedes

Look out!

Goannas and snakes running away from the floods have climbed the same tree.

Below, a water python catches a dusky rat while a king brown snake slithers into the bushes.

Kakadu has many waterfalls. Some flow all year round, others only during the wet season. It is the force of these waterfalls that has slowly eroded the deep waterholes that keep Kakadu alive during the Dry.

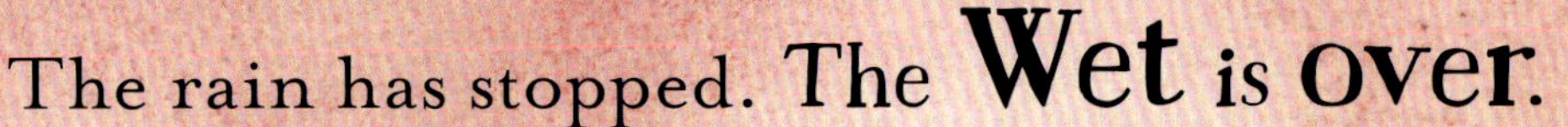
The rain has stopped. The **Wet** is **over.**

Under clear blue skies, mists blanket the wetlands each morning. Dragonflies zip across the pools and lakes, which are beginning to shrink. Migratory birds leave Kakadu, the great flights of little curlews and snipes darkening the air.

The wetlands are a carpet of waterlilies, their flowers held up from the lily pads on long, slender stems.

The wetlands are home to many species of plants, including waterlilies. Leaf pondweed, sedges and spike rush live in the water. Around the billabongs grow freshwater mangroves, pandanus and forests of paperbarks, and under these the agile wallaby grazes.

Now the wind storms come, **surging and gusting**. "Knock 'em down" storms flatten the tall spear grass to the ground, where it is eaten by wallabies, or swiftly taken for nests by birds and termites.

Green tree ants build a new nest by sticking leaves together. Inside it they will farm other insects to collect their honeydew.

There are countless species of insects living in Kakadu. From tiny mosquito larvae living in ponds to the large Leichhardt's grasshopper, from damsel flies to dragonflies, from green tree ants to termites, every part of Kakadu is alive.

The sun burns down. The floods recede, leaving rich soil behind for new growth. Creeks retreat into their beds and the waterholes sink down.

The northern long-necked turtle buries itself in mud on the riverbank.

This is the **Dry.**
Now, Kakadu waits for the **Wet.**

It will come, as it always does.

About Kakadu

Kakadu is Australia's largest national park – over 20,000 square kilometres. It is dual World Heritage-listed for its extraordinary natural and cultural value. It covers a wide range of habitats and ecosystems, from beaches to the Arnhem Plateau to the wetlands to the dry centre. All are shaped by the yearly cycle of wet and dry seasons.

Kakadu is Aboriginal land. It is leased by its traditional owners, the Bininj and Mungguy people, to the Director of National Parks so it can be jointly managed. There is much more to Kakadu than landscape and animals – it is a site of great cultural importance where, for example, you can see rock paintings that date back 20,000 years. It is estimated that Aboriginal people have lived in Kakadu for up to 65,000 years – the oldest living culture on earth.

Kakadu's native species have been endangered by the introduced cane toad (which is poisonous if eaten) and feral predators such as cats and foxes. Much of the park staff's work is devoted to ensuring that native species are protected.

Although cycles of Wet and Dry have been stable for centuries, there is some evidence that climate change is shifting the patterns of monsoon rainfall. We do not know what effect this will have on the environment of Kakadu.

This picture book has discussed two main seasons, the Wet and the Dry, but the Indigenous people of Kakadu know that there are actually six seasons: Wurrgeng, Gurrung, Gunumeleng, Gudjewg, Banggerreng and Yegge.

Wurrgeng: Cold weather season (but it's still 30°C in the day!). Mid-June to mid-August. **Pages 2–3**

Gurrung: Hot, dry weather. Mid-August to mid-October. **Pages 4–5**

Gunumeleng: Pre-monsoon storm season. Mid-October to late December. **Pages 6–13**

Gudjewg: Monsoon season (the Wet arrives). December to March. **Pages 14–21**

Banggerreng: "Knock 'em down" storm season. April. **Pages 22–25**

Yegge: Dry and cooler, but still humid. May to mid-June. **Pages 26–27**

Map of Kakadu

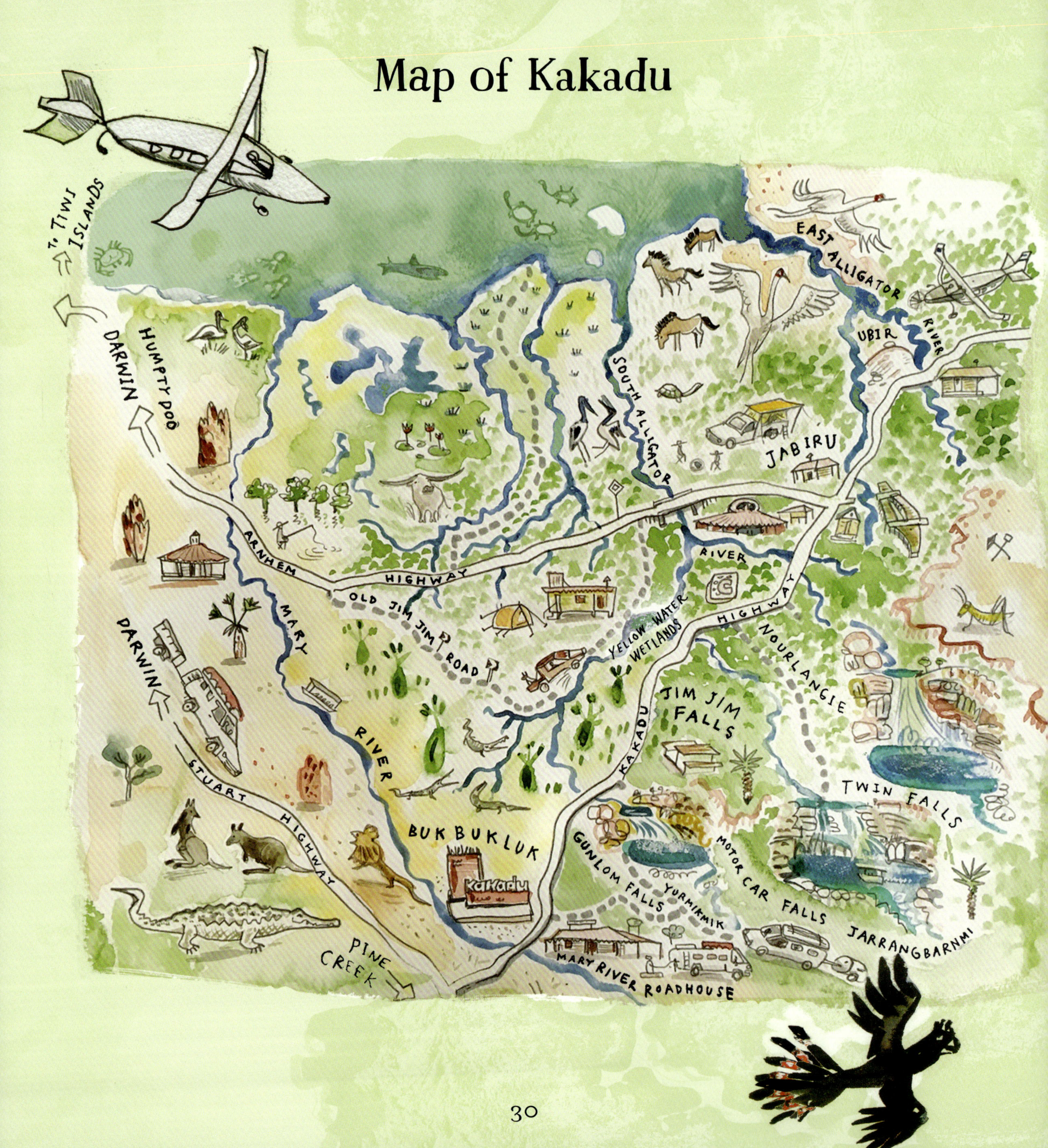

Look up the pages to find out all about Kakadu, its seasons and its wildlife. Don't forget to look at both kinds of words – this kind and **this kind.**

Index

Aboriginal 28
agile wallaby 23
Arctic Circle 4
Banggerreng 29
banyan tree 10
billabong 8, 9, 23
Bininj people 28
bird 5, 10, 17, 19, 22, 24
creek 3, 19, 26
crocodile 3, 17
crustacean 17
curlew 22
damsel fly 25
dragonflies 25
the Dry 2, 21, 26, 29
eel 10
estuaries 17
fish 9, 10, 17
frog 10, 17, 19, 20
gecko 12
goanna 20
godwit 4
green tree ant 25
Gudjewg 29
Gunumeleng 29
Gurrung 29
humidity 15
Indigenous 29
Kakadu 28, 29
Leichhardt's Grasshopper 5, 25
long-legged jabiru 10
magpie lark 8
mangrove 23
migratory birds 22
monsoon 14, 15, 28, 29
Mungguy people 28
northern Australia 2, 3
northern long-necked turtle 3, 26
pandanus 23
paperbark 20, 23
Pityrodia bush 5
plateau 20, 28
rain 7, 14, 15, 19, 22
red lily 8
red-tailed black cockatoo 6
river 2, 3, 4, 17, 19, 26, 29
seasons 3, 15, 18, 21, 28, 29
sharp-tailed sandpipers 4
snakes 10, 19, 20
snipe 4, 22
spear grass 18, 24
species 5, 10, 23, 25, 28
spring 9
storms 6, 7, 24, 29
summer 9, 12, 14
termite 12, 13, 24, 25
termite mound 12, 13
waterfall 20, 21
waterlilies 23
the Wet 3, 22, 26, 29
wetland 23, 28
Wurrgeng 29
Yegge 29
Yellow Water wetlands 6

To the native water rats who have figured out how to safely eat cane toads – PF

To Sarah Davis, art director of tireless encouragement – LA

First published in 2020
by Walker Books Australia Pty Ltd
Locked Bag 22, Newtown
NSW 2042 Australia
www.walkerbooks.com.au

This edition published in 2023.

EU Authorized Representative: HackettFlynn Ltd,
36 Cloch Choirneal, Balrothery, Co. Dublin, K32 C942, Ireland.
EU@walkerpublishinggroup.com

A catalogue record for this book is available from the National Library of Australia

ISBN 978 1 760656 23 2

The illustrations for this book were created with mixed media
Typeset in Mrs Eaves and Mrs Ant
Printed and bound in China

10 9 8 7 6 5